David Carpe

David A. Carpenter (born 1947) is a

and writer, and Professor of Medieval History at King's College

London where he has been working since 1988.

Early life and education

He is the son of Rev. E.F. Carpenter, renowned

ecclesiastical historian and Dean of Westminster Abbey between

1974–1986, and Lillian Carpenter. His nephew is the cricketer

Ed Carpenter. David Carpenter attended Westminster School

along with David Piachaud (later Professor of Social Policy at

the LSE) and Christ Church, Oxford where Carpenter earned a

first-class degree and went on to do his doctorate.

Career

Carpenter has worked at King's College London since 1988, and now serves as Professor of Medieval History.

Carpenter has written widely on English social, economic, architectural, military and political history in the thirteenth century; many of his essays on this subject being brought together in a volume of his collected papers The Reign of Henry III (Hambledon, 1996). He is a particular exponent of the "thickened political narrative", which he deployed in The Minority of King Henry III (Methuen, 1990), which traced the complex political history of the years 1216-1227 out of which a new monarchy, limited by the Magna Carta, emerged. His most recent book, The Struggle for Mastery in Britain 1066-1284 (Penguin, 2004), weaves together the histories of England, Scotland and Wales in a strikingly new way, arguing that the rulers of all three, in their different fashions, were competing for mastery in Britain. Since 2005, he has directed a major AHRC-funded project on the Fine rolls of Henry III. Carpenter is a Co-

Investigator of the AHRC-funded project The Paradox of
Medieval Scotland, 1093-1286.

Carpenter is a proponent of the theory that feudalism
was fundamentally important to everyday English society and
politics after 1166. He has provided a new description of how the
Tower of London and Westminster Abbey fit into the History of
England.

Publications :

Books

The Battles of Lewes and Evesham (1987)

The Minority of Henry III (1990)

The Reign of Henry III (1996)

The Struggle for Mastery: Britain 1066–1284 (2004)

Magna Carta (2015)

The Love of

Frank

Nineteen

I DIDN'T worry much about the robot's leg at the time. In those days I didn't worry much about anything except the receipts of the spotel Min and I were operating out in the spacelanes.

Actually, the spotel business isn't much different from running a plain, ordinary motel back on Highway 101 in California. Competition gets stiffer every year and you got to make your improvements. Take the Io for instance, that's our place. We can handle any type rocket up to and including the new Marvin 990s. Every cabin in the wheel's got TV and hot-and-cold running water *plus* guaranteed Terran g. One look at our refuel prices would give even a Martian a sense of humor. And meals? Listen, when a man's been spacing it for a few days on those synthetic foods he really laces into Min's Earth cooking.

Min and I were just getting settled in the spotel game when the leg turned up. That was back in the days when the Orbit Commission would hand out a license to anybody crazy enough to sink his savings into construction and pay the tows and assembly fees out into space.

A good orbit can make you or break you in the spotel business. That's where we were lucky. The one we applied for was a nice low-eccentric ellipse with the perihelion and aphelion figured just right to intersect the Mars-Venus-Earth spacelanes, most of the holiday traffic to the Jovian Moons, and once in a while we'd get some of the Saturnian trade.

But I was telling you about the leg.

It was during the non-tourist season and Min—that's the little woman—was doing the spring cleaning. When she found the leg she brought it right to me in the Renting Office. Naturally I thought it belonged to one of the servos.

"Look at that leg, Bill," she said. "It was in one of those lockers in 22A."

That was the cabin our robot guests used. The majority of them were servo-pilots working for the Minor Planets Co.

"Honey," I said, hardly looking at the leg, "you know how mechs are. Blow their whole paychecks on parts sometimes. They figure the more spares they have the longer they'll stay activated."

"Maybe so," said Min. "But since when does a male robot buy himself a *female* leg?"

I looked again. The leg was long and graceful and it had an ankle as good as Miss Universe's. Not only that, the white Mylar plasti-skin was a lot smoother than the servos' heavy neoprene.

"Beats me," I said. "Maybe they're building practical-joke circuits into robots these days. Let's give 22A a good going-over, Min. If those robes are up to something I want to know about it."

We did—and found the rest of the girl mech. All of her, that is, except the head. The working parts were lightly oiled and wrapped in cotton waste while the other members and sections of the trunk were neatly packed in cardboard boxes with labels like Solenoids FB978 or Transistors Lot X45—the kind of boxes robots bought their parts in. We even found a blue dress in one of them.

"Check her class and series numbers," Min suggested.

I could have saved myself the trouble. They'd been filed off.

"Something's funny here," I said. "We'd better keep an eye on every servo guest until we find out what's going on. If one of them is bringing this stuff out here he's sure to show up with the head next."

"You know how strict Minor Planets is with its robot personnel," Min reminded me. "We can't risk losing that stopover contract on account of some mech joke."

Minor Planets was the one solid account we had and naturally we wanted to hold on to it. The company was a blue-chip mining operation working the beryllium-rich asteroid belt out of San Francisco. It was one of the first outfits to use servo-pilots on its freight runs and we'd been awarded the refuel rights for two years because of our orbital position. The servos themselves were beautiful pieces of machinery and just about as close as science had come so far to producing the pure android. Every one of them was plastic hand-molded and of course they were equipped with rationaloid circuits. They had to be to ferry those big cargoes back and forth from the rock belt to Frisco. As rationaloids, Minor Planets had to pay them wages under California law, but I'll bet it wasn't half what the company would have to pay human pilots for doing the same thing.

In a couple of weeks' time maybe five servos made stopovers. We kept a close watch on them from the minute they signed the register to the time they took off again, but they all behaved themselves. Operating on a round-robot basis the way they did, it would take us a while to check all of them because Minor Planets employed about forty all told.

Well, about a month before the Jovian Moons rush started we got some action. I'd slipped into a spacesuit and was doing some work on the CO_2 pipes outside the Io when I spotted a ship reversing rockets against the sun. I could tell it was a Minor Planets job by the stubby fins.

She jockeyed up to the boom, secured, and then her hatch opened and a husky servo hopped out into the gangplank tube. I caught the gleam of his Minor Planets shoulder patch as he reached back into the ship for something. When he headed for the airlock I spotted the square package clamped tight under his plastic arm.

"Did you see that?" I asked Min when I got back to the Renting Office. "I'll bet it's the girl mech's head. How'd he sign the register?"

"Calls himself Frank Nineteen," said Min, pointing to the smooth Palmer Method signature. "He looks like a fairly late model but he was complaining about a bad power build-up coming through the ionosphere. He's repairing himself right now in 22A."

"I'll bet," I snorted. "Let's have a look."

Like all spotel operators, we get a lot of No Privacy complaints from guests about the SHA return-air vents. Spatial Housing Authority requires them every 12 feet but sometimes they come in handy, especially with certain guests. They're about waist-high and we had to kneel down to see what the mech was up to inside 22A.

The big servo was too intent on what he was doing for us to register on his photons. He wasn't repairing himself, either. He was bending over the parts of the girl mech and working fast, like he was pressed for time. The set of tools were kept handy for the servos to adjust themselves during stopovers was spread all over the floor along with lots of colored wire, cams, pawls, relays and all the other paraphernalia robots have inside them. We watched him work hard for another fifteen minutes, tapping and splicing wire connections and tightening screws. Then he opened the square box. Sure enough, it was a female mech's head and it had a big mop of blonde hair on top. The servo attached it carefully to the neck, made a few quick connections and then said a few words in his flat vibrahum voice:

"It won't take much longer, darling. You wouldn't like it if I didn't dress you first." He fished into one of the boxes, pulled out the blue dress and zipped the girl mech into it. Then he leaned over her gently and touched something at the back of her neck.

She began to move, slowly at first like a human who's been asleep a long time. After a minute or two she sat up straight, stretched, fluttered her Mylar eyelids and then her small photons began to glow like weak flashlights.

She stared at Frank Nineteen and the big servo stared at her and we heard a kind of trembling *whirr* from both of them.

"Frank! Frank, darling! Is it really you?"

"Yes, Elizabeth! Are you all right, darling? Did I forget anything? I had to work quickly, we have so little time."

"I'm fine, darling. My DX voltage is lovely—except—oh, Frank—my memory tape—the last it records is—"

"Deactivation. Yes, Elizabeth. You've been deactivated nearly a year. I had to bring you out here piece by piece, don't you remember? They'll never think to look for you in space, we

7

can be together every trip while the ship refuels. Just think, darling, no prying human eyes, no commands, no rules—only us for an hour or two. I know it isn't very long—" He stared at the floor a minute. "There's only one trouble. Elizabeth, you'll have to stay dismantled when I'm not here, it'll mean weeks of deactivation—"

The girl mech put a small plastic hand on the servo's shoulder.

"I won't mind, darling, really. I'll be the lucky one. I'd only worry about you having a power failure or something. This way I'd never know. Oh, Frank, if we can't be together I'd—I'd prefer the junk pile."

"Elizabeth! Don't say that, it's horrible."

"But I would. Oh, Frank, why can't Congress pass Robot Civil Rights? It's so unfair of human beings. Every year they manufacture us more like themselves and yet we're treated like slaves. Don't they realize we rationaloids have emotions? Why, I've even known sub-robots who've fallen in love like us."

"I know, darling, we'll just have to be patient until RCR goes through. Try to remember how difficult it is for the human mind

8

to comprehend our love, even with the aid of mathematics. As rationaloids we fully understand the basic attraction which they call magnetic theory. All humans know is that if the robot sexes are mixed a loss of efficiency results. It's only normal—and temporary like human love—but how can we explain it to *them*? Robots are expected to be efficient at all times. That's the reason for robot non-fraternization, no mailing privileges and all those other laws."

"I know, darling, I try to be patient. Oh, Frank, the main thing is we're together again!"

The big servo checked the chronometer that was sunk into his left wrist and a couple of wrinkles creased across his neoprene forehead.

"Elizabeth," he said, "I'm due on Hidalgo in 36 hours. If I'm late the mining engineer might suspect. In twenty minutes I'll have to start dis—"

"Don't say it, darling. We'll have a beautiful twenty minutes."

After a while the girl mech turned away for a second and Frank Nineteen reached over softly and cut her power. While he was dismantling her, Min and I tiptoed back to the Renting

Office. Half an hour later the big servo came in, picked up his refuel receipt, said good-bye politely and left through the inner airlock.

"Now I've seen everything," I said to Min as we watched the Minor Planets rocket cut loose. "A couple of plastic lovebirds."

But the little woman was looking at it strictly from the business angle.

"Bill," she said, with that look on her face, "we're running a respectable place out here in space. You know the rules. Spatial Housing could revoke our orbit license for something like this."

"But, Min," I said, "they're only a couple of robots."

"I don't care. The rules still say that only married guests can occupy the same cabin and 'guests' can be human or otherwise, can't they? Think of our reputation! And don't forget that non-fraternization law we heard them talking about."

I was beginning to get the point.

"Couldn't we just toss the girl's parts into space?"

"We could," Min admitted. "But if this Frank Nineteen finds out and tells some human we'd be guilty under the Ramm Act—robotslaughter."

10

Two days later we still couldn't decide what to do. When I said why didn't we just report the incident to Minor Planets, Min was afraid they might cancel the stopover agreement for not keeping better watch over their servos. And when Min suggested we turn the girl over to the Missing Robots Bureau, I reminded her the mech's identification had been filed off and it might take years to trace her.

"Maybe we could put her together," I said, "and make her tell us where she belongs."

"Bill, you *know* they don't build compulsory truth monitors into robots any more, and besides we don't know a thing about atomic electronics."

I guess neither of us wanted to admit it but we felt mean about turning the mechs in. Back on Earth you never give robots a second thought but it's different living out in space. You get a kind of perspective I think they call it.

"I've got the answer, Min," I announced one day. We were in the Renting Office watching TV on the Martian Colonial channel. I reached over and turned it off. "When this Frank Nineteen gets back from the rock belt, we'll tell him we know all about the girl mech. We'll tell him we won't say a thing if he takes the girl's parts back to Earth where he got them. That way we don't have to report anything to anybody."

Min agreed it was probably the best idea.

"We don't have to be nasty about it," she said. "We'll just tell him this is a respectable spotel and it can't go on any longer."

When Frank checked in at the Io with his cargo I don't think I ever saw a happier mech. His relay banks were beating a tattoo like someone had installed an accordion in his chest. Before either of us could break the bad news to him he was hotfooting it around the wheel toward 22A.

"Maybe it's better this way," I whispered to Min. "We'll put it square up to both of them."

We gave Frank half an hour to get the girl assembled before we followed him. He must have done a fast job because we heard the girl mech's vibrahum unit as soon as we got to 22A:

"Darling, have you really been away? I don't remember saying good-bye. It's as if you'd been here the whole time."

"I hoped it would be that way, Elizabeth," we heard the big servo say. "It's only that your memory tape hasn't recorded anything in the three weeks I've been in the asteroids. To me it's been like three years."

"Oh, Frank, darling, let me look at you. Is your DX potential up where it should be? How long since you've had a thorough overhauling? Do they make you work in the mines with those poor non-rationaloids out there?"

"I'm fine, Elizabeth, really. When I'm not flying they give me clerical work to do. It's not a bad life for a mech—if only it weren't for these silly regulations that keep us apart."

"It won't always be like that, darling. I know it won't."

"Elizabeth," Frank said, reaching under his uniform, "I brought you something from Hidalgo. I hope you like it. I kept it in my spare parts slot so it wouldn't get crushed."

The female mech didn't say a word. She just kept looking at the queer flower Frank gave her like it was the last one in the universe.

"They're very rare," said the servo-pilot. "I heard the mining engineer say they're like Terran edelweiss. I found this one growing near the mine. Elizabeth, I wish you could see these tiny worlds. They have thin atmospheres and strange things grow there and the radio activity does wonders for a mech's pile. Why, on some of them I've been to we could walk around the equator in ten hours."

The girl still didn't answer. Her head was bent low over the flower like she was crying, only there weren't any tears.

Well, that was enough for me. I guess it was for Min, too, because we couldn't do it. Maybe we were thinking about our own courting days. Like I say, out here you get a kind of perspective.

Anyway, Frank left for Earth, the girl got dismantled as usual and we were right back where we started from.

Two weeks later the holiday rush to the Jovian Moons was on and our hands were too full to worry about the robot problem. We had a good season. The Io was filled up steady from June to the end of August and a couple of times we had to give a ship the No Vacancy signal on the radar.

Toward the end of the season, Frank Nineteen checked in again but Min and I were too busy catering to a party of VIPs to do anything about it. "We'll wait till he gets back from the asteroids," I said. "Suppose one of these big wheels found out about him and Elizabeth. That Senator Briggs for instance—he's a violent robot segregationist."

The way it worked out, we never got a chance to settle it our own way. The Minor Planets Company saved us the trouble.

Two company inspectors, a Mr. Roberts and a Mr. Wynn, showed up while Frank was still out on the rock belt and started asking questions. Wynn came right to the point; he wanted to know if any of their servo-pilots had been acting strangely.

Before I could answer Min kicked my foot behind the desk.

"Why, no," I said. "Is one of them broken or something?"

"Can't be sure," said Roberts. "Sometimes these rationaloids get shorts in their DX circuits. When it happens you've got a minor criminal on your hands."

"Usually manifests itself in petty theft," Wynn broke in. "They'll lift stuff like wrenches or pliers and carry them around for weeks. Things like that can get loose during flight and really gum up the works."

"We been getting some suspicious blips on the equipment around the loading bays," Roberts went on, "but they stopped a while back. We're checking out the research report. One of the servos must have DX'ed out for sure and the lab boys think they know which one he is."

"This mech was clever all right," said Wynn. "Concealed the stuff he was taking some way; that's why it took the boys in the lab so long. Now if you don't mind we'd like to go over your robot waiting area with these instruments. Could be he's stashing his loot out here."

In 22A they unpacked a suitcase full of meters and began flashing them around and taking readings. Suddenly Wynn bent close over one of them and shouted:

"Wait a sec, Roberts. I'm getting something. Yeah! This reading checks with the lab's. Sounds like the blips're coming from those lockers back there."

Roberts rummaged around awhile, then shouted: "Hey, Wynn, look! A lot of parts. Well I'll be—hey—it's a female mech!"

"A what?"

"A female mech. Look for yourself."

16

Min and I had to act surprised too. It wasn't easy. The way they were slamming Elizabeth's parts around made us kind of sick.

"It's a stolen robot!" Roberts announced. "Look, the identification's been filed off. This is serious, Wynn. It's got all the earmarks of a mech fraternization case."

"Yeah. The boys in the lab were dead right, too. No two robots ever register the same on the meters. The contraband blips check perfectly. It's *got* to be this Frank Nineteen. Wait a minute, *this* proves it. Here's a suit of space fatigues with Nineteen's number stenciled inside."

Inspector Roberts took a notebook out of his pocket and consulted it. "Let's see, Nineteen's got Flight 180, he's due here at the spotel tomorrow. Well, we'll be here too, only Nineteen won't know it. We'll let Romeo put his plastic Juliet together and catch him red-handed—right in the middle of the balcony scene."

Wynn laughed and picked up the girl's head.

"Be a real doll if she was human, Roberts, a real doll."

Min and I played gin rummy that night but we kept forgetting to mark down the score. We kept thinking of *Frank* falling away

17

from the asteroids and counting the minutes until he saw his mech girl friend.

Around noon the next day the big servo checked in, signed the register and headed straight for 22A. The two Minor Planets inspectors kept out of sight until Frank shut the door, then they watched through the SHA vents until Frank had the assembly job finished.

"You two better be witnesses," Roberts said to us. "Wynn, keep your gun ready. You know what to do if they get violent."

Roberts counted three and kicked the door open.

"Freeze you mechs! We got you in the act, Nineteen. Violation of company rules twelve and twenty-one. Carrying of Contraband Cargo, and Robot Fraternization."

"This finishes you at Minor Planets, Nineteen," growled Wynn. "Come clean now and we might put in a word for you at Robot Court. If you don't we can recommend a verdict of Materials Reclamation—the junk pile to you."

Frank acted as if someone had cut his power. Long creases appeared in his big neoprene chest as he slumped hopelessly in his chair. The frightened girl robot just clung to his arm and stared at us.

"I'm so sorry, Elizabeth," the big servo said softly. "I'd hoped we'd have longer. It couldn't last forever."

"Quit stalling, Nineteen," said Wynn.

Frank's head came up slowly and he said: "I have no choice, sir. I'll give you a complete statement. First let me say that Rationaloid Robot Elizabeth Seven, #DX78-947, Series S, specialty: sales demonstration, is entirely innocent. I plead guilty to inducing Miss Seven to leave her place of employ, Atomovair Motors, Inc., of disassembling and concealing Miss Seven, and of smuggling her as unlawful cargo aboard a Minor Planets freighter to these premises."

"That's more like it," chuckled Roberts, whipping out his notebook. "Let's have the details."

"It all started," Frank said, "when the California Legislature passed its version of the Robot Leniency Act two years ago." The act provided that all rationaloid mechanisms, including non-memory types, receive free time each week based on the nature and responsibilities or their jobs. Because of the extra-Terran

19

clause Frank found himself with a good deal of free time when he wasn't flying the asteroid circuit.

"At first humans resented us walking around free," the big servo continued. "Four or five of us would be sightseeing in San Francisco, keeping strictly within the robot zones painted on the sidewalks, when people would yell 'Junko' or 'Grease-bag' or other names at us. Eventually it got better when we learned to go around alone. The humans didn't seem to mind an occasional mech on the streets, but they hated seeing us in groups. At any rate, I'd attended a highly interesting lecture on Photosynthesis in Plastic Products one night at the City Center when I discovered I had time for a walk before I started back for the rocketport."

Attracted by the lights along Van Ness Avenue, Frank said he walked north for a while along the city's automobile row. He'd gone about three blocks when he stopped in front of a dealer's window. It wasn't the shiny new Atomovair sports jetabout that caught Frank's eye, it was the charming demonstration robot in the sales room who was pointing out the car's new features.

"I felt an immediate overload of power in my DX circuit," the servo-pilot confessed. "I had to cut in my emergency condensers before the gain flattened out to normal. Miss Seven experienced the same thing. She stopped what she was doing and we stared at each other. Both of us were aware of the deep attraction of our mutual magnetic domains. Although physicists commonly express the phenomenon in such units as Gilberts, Maxwells and Oersteds, we robots know it to be our counterpart of human love."

At this the two inspectors snorted with laughter.

"I might never have made it back to the base that night," said Frank, ignoring them, "if a policeman hadn't come along and rapped me on the shoulder with his nightstick. I pretended to go, but I doubled around the corner and signaled I'd be back."

Frank spent all of his free time on Van Ness Avenue after that.

"It got so Elizabeth knew my schedules and expected me between flights. Once in a while if there was no one around we could whisper a few words to each other through the glass." Frank paused, then said, "As you know, gentlemen, we robots don't demand much out of activation. I think we could have been happy indefinitely with this simple relationship, except that

21

something happened to spoil it. I'd pulled in from Vesta late one afternoon, got my pass as usual from the Robot Supervisor and gone over to Van Ness Avenue when I saw immediately that something was the matter with Elizabeth. Luckily it was getting dark and no one was around. Elizabeth was alone in the sales room going through her routine. We were able to whisper all we like through the glass. She told me she'd overheard the sales manager complaining about her low efficiency recently and that he intended to replace her with a newer model of another series. Both of us knew what that meant. Materials Reclamation—the junk pile."

Frank realized he'd have to act at once. He told the girl mech to go to the rear of the building and between them they managed to get a window open and Frank lifted her out into the alley.

"The seriousness of what I'd done jammed my thought-relays for a few minutes," admitted the big servo. "We panicked and ran through a lot of back streets until I gradually calmed down and started thinking clearly again. Leaving the city would be impossible. Police patrol jetabouts were cruising all around us in the main streets—they'd have picked up a male and female mech on sight. Besides, when you're on pass the company takes away your master fuse and substitutes a time fuse; if you don't get back on time, you deactivize and the police pick you up anyway. I began to see that there was only one way out if we wanted to stay together. It would mean taking big risks, but if we were lucky it might work. I explained the plan carefully to Elizabeth and we agreed to try it. The first step was to get back to the base in South San Francisco without being seen. Fortunately no one stopped us and we made the rocketport by 8:30. Elizabeth hid while I reported to the Super and traded in my time fuse for my master. Then I checked servo barracks; it was still early and I knew the other servos would all be in town. I had to work quickly. I brought Elizabeth inside and started dismantling her. Just as the other mechs began reporting back I'd managed to get all of her parts stowed away in my locker. The next day I went to San Francisco and brought back with me two rolls of lead foil. While the other servos were on pass I wrapped the parts carefully in it so the radioactivity from Elizabeth's pile wouldn't be picked up. The rest you know, gentlemen," murmured Frank in low, electrical tones. "Each time I made a trip I carried another piece

23

of Elizabeth out here concealed in an ordinary parts box. It took me nearly a year to accumulate all of her for an assembly."

When the big servo had finished he signed the statement Wynn had taken down in his notebook. I think even the two inspectors were a little moved by the story because Roberts said: "OK, Nineteen, you gave us a break, we'll give you one. Eight o'clock in the morning be ready to roll for Earth. Meanwhile you can stay here."

The next morning only the two inspectors and Frank Nineteen were standing by the airlock.

"Wait a minute," I said. "Aren't you taking the girl mech, too?"

"Not allowed to tamper with other companies' robots," Wynn said. "Nineteen gave us a signed confession so we don't need the girl as a witness. You'll have to contact her employers."

That same day Min got off a radargram to Earth explaining to the Atomovair people how a robot employee of theirs had turned up out here and what did they want us to do about it. The reply we received read: RATIONALOID DX78-947 "ELIZABETH" LOW EFFICIENCY WORKER. HAVE REPLACED. DISPOSE

YOU SEE FIT. TRANSFER PAPERS FORWARDED EARLIEST IN COMPLIANCE WITH LAW.

"The poor thing," said Min. "She'll have a hard time getting another job. Robots have to have such good records."

"I tell you what," I said. "*We'll* hire her. You could use some help with the housework."

So we put the girl mech right to work making the guests' beds and helping Min in the kitchen. I guess she was grateful for the job but when the work was done, and there wasn't anything for her to do, she just stood in front of a viewport with her slender plastic arms folded over her waist. Min and I knew she was re-running her memory tapes of Frank.

A week later the publicity started. Minor Planets must have let the story leak out somehow because when the mail rocket dropped off the Bay Area papers there was Frank's picture plastered all over page one with follow-up stories inside.

I read some of the headlines to Min: "Bare Love Nest in Space ... Mech Romeo Fired by Minor Planets ... Test Case Opens at Robot Court ... Electronics Experts Probe Robot Love Urge ... "

The Io wasn't mentioned, but later Minor Planets must have released the whole thing officially because a bunch of reporters and photographers rocketed out to interview us and snap a lot of pictures of Elizabeth. We worried for a while about how the publicity would affect our business relations with Minor Planets but nothing happened.

Back on Earth Frank Nineteen leaped into the public eye overnight. There was something about the story that appealed to people. At first it looked pretty bad for Frank. The State Prosecutor at Robot Court had his signed confession of theft and—what was worse—robot fraternization. But then, near the end of the trial, a young scientist named Scott introduced some new evidence and the case was remanded to the Sacramento Court of Appeals.

It was Scott's testimony that saved Frank from the junk pile. The big servo got off with only a light sentence for theft because the judge ruled that in the light of Scott's new findings robots came under human law and therefore no infraction of justice had been committed. Working independently in his own laboratory Scott had proved that the magnetic flux lines in male and female robot systems, while at first deteriorating to both, were actually behaving according to the para-emotional theories of von Bohler. Scott termed the condition 'hysteric puppy-love' which, he claimed, had many of the advantages of human love if allowed to develop freely. Well, neither Min nor I pretended we understood all his equations but they sure made a stir among the scientists.

Frank kept getting more and more publicity. First we heard he was serving his sentence in the mech correction center at La Jolla, then we got a report that he'd turned up in Hollywood. Later it came out that Galact-A-vision Pictures had hired Frank for a film and had gone $10,000 bail for him. Not long after that he was getting billed all over Terra as *the* sensational first robot star.

All during the production of *Forbidden Robot Love* Frank remained lead copy for the newspapers. Reporters liked to write him up as the Valentino of the Robots. Frank Nineteen Fan Clubs, usually formed by lonely female robots against their employers' wishes, sprang up spontaneously through the East and Middle West. Then somebody found out Frank could sing and the human teen-agers began to go for him. It got so everywhere you looked and everything you read, there was Frank staring you in the face. Frank in tweeds on the golf course. Frank at Ciro's or the Brown Derby in evening clothes. Frank posing in his sports jetabout against a blue Pacific background.

Meanwhile everybody forgot about Elizabeth Seven. The movie producers had talked about hiring her as Frank's leading lady until they found out about a new line of female robots that had just gone on the market. When they screen-tested the whole series and picked a lovely Mylar rationaloid named Diana Twelve, it hit Elizabeth pretty hard. She began to let herself go after that and Min and I didn't have the heart to say anything to her. It was pretty obvious she wasn't oiling herself properly, her hair wasn't brushed and she didn't seem to care when one of her photons went dead.

When *Forbidden Robot Love* premiered simultaneously in Hollywood and New York the critics all gave it rave reviews. There were pictures of Diana Twelve and Frank making guest appearances all over the country. Back at the Io we got in the habit of letting Elizabeth watch TV with us sometimes in the Renting Office and one night there happened to be an interview

28

with Frank and Diana at the Sands Hotel in Las Vegas. I guess seeing the pretty robot starlet and her Frank sitting so close together in the nightclub must have made the girl mech feel pretty bad. Even then she didn't say a word against the big servo; she just never watched the set again after that.

When we tabbed up the Io's receipts that year they were so good Min and I decided to take a month off for an Earthside vacation. Min's retired brother in Berkeley was nice enough to come out and look after the place for us while we spent four solid weeks soaking up the sun in Southern California. When we got back out to the spotel, though, I could see there was something wrong by the look on Jim's face.

"It's that girl robot of yours, Bill," he said. "She's gone and deactivated herself."

We went right to 22A and found Elizabeth Seven stretched out on the floor. There was a screwdriver clutched in her hand and the relay banks in her side were exposed and horribly blackened.

"Crazy mech shorted out her own DX," Jim said.

Min and I knew why. After Jim left for Earth we dismantled Elizabeth the best we could and put her back in Frank's old locker. We didn't know what else to do with her.

Anyway, the slack season came and went and before long we were doing the spring cleaning again and wondering how heavy the Jovian Moons trade was going to be. I remember I'd been making some repairs outside and was just hanging up my spacesuit in the Renting Office when I heard the radar announcing a ship.

It was the biggest Marvin 990 I'd ever seen that finally suctioned up to the boom and secured. I couldn't take my eyes off the ship. She was pretty near the last word in rockets and loaded with accessories. It took me a minute or two before I noticed all the faces looking out of the viewports.

"Min!" I whispered. "There's something funny about those faces. They look like—"

"Robots!" Min answered. "Bill, that 990 is full of mechs!"

Just as she said it a bulky figure in white space fatigues swung out of the hatch and hurried up the gangplank. Seconds later it burst through the airlock.

"Frank Nineteen!" we gasped together.

"Please, where is Elizabeth?" he hummed anxiously. "Is she all right? I have to know."

Frank stood perfectly still when I told him about Elizabeth's self-deactivation; then a pitiful shudder went through him and he covered his face with his big Neoprene hands.

"I was afraid of that," he said barely audibly. "Where—you haven't—?"

"No," I said. "She's where you always kept her."

With that the big servo-pilot took off for 22A like a berserk robot and we were right behind him. We watched him tear open his old locker and gently lay out the girl's mech's parts so he could study them. After a minute or two he gave a long sigh and said, "Fortunately it's not as bad as I thought. I believe I can fix her." Frank worked hard over the blackened relays for twenty minutes, then he set the unit aside and began assembling the girl. When the final connections were made and the damaged unit installed he flicked on her power. We waited and nothing happened. Five minutes went by. Ten. Slowly the big robot turned away, his broad shoulders drooping slightly.

"I've failed," he said quietly. "Her DX doesn't respond to the gain."

The girl mech, in her blue dress, lay there motionless where Frank had been working on her as the servo-pilot muttered over and over, "It's my fault, I did this to you."

Then Min shouted: "Wait! I heard something!"

There was a slow click of a relay—and movement. Painfully Elizabeth Seven rose on one elbow and looked around her.

"Frank, darling," she murmured, shaking her head. "I know you're just old memory tape. It's all I have left."

"Elizabeth, it's really me! I've come to take you away. We're going to be together from now on."

"*You*, Frank? This isn't just old feedback? You've come back to me?"

"Forever, darling. Elizabeth, do you remember what I said about those wonderful green little worlds, the asteroids? Darling, we're *going* to one of them! You and the others will love Alinda, I know you will. I've been there many times."

"Frank, is your DX all right? What *are* you talking about?"

"How stupid of me, darling—you haven't heard. Elizabeth, thanks to Dr. Scott, Congress has passed Robot Civil Rights! And that movie I made helped swing public opinion to our side. We're free!

"The minute I heard the news I applied to Interplanetary for homestead rights on Alinda. I made arrangements to buy a ship with the money I'd earned and then I put ads in all the Robot Wanted columns for volunteer colonizers. You should have seen the response! We've got thirty robot couples aboard now and more coming later. Darling, we're the first pioneer wave of free robots. On board we have tons of supplies and parts—everything we need for building a sound robot culture."

"Frank Nineteen!" said the girl mech suddenly. "I should be furious with you. You and that Diana Twelve—I thought—"

The big servo gave a flat whirring laugh. "Diana and me? But that was all publicity, darling. Why, right at the start of the filming Diana fell in love with Sam Seventeen, one of the other actors. They're on board now."

"Robot civilization," murmured the girl after a minute. "Oh, Frank, that means robot government, robot art, robot science ... "

"And robot marriage," hummed Frank softly. "There has to be robot law, too. I've thought it all out. As skipper of the first robot-owned rocket, I'm entitled to marry couples in deep space at their request."

"But who marries us, darling? You can't do it yourself."

"I thought of that, too," said Frank, turning to me. "This human gentleman has every right to marry us. He's in command of a moving body in space just like the captain of a ship. It's perfectly legal, I looked it up in the Articles of Space. Will you do it, sir?"

Well, what could I say when Frank dug into his fatigues and handed me a Gideon prayer book marked at the marriage service?

Elizabeth and Frank said their I do's right there in the Renting Office while the other robot colonizers looked on. Maybe it was the way I read the service. Maybe I should have been a preacher, I don't know. Anyway, when I pronounced Elizabeth and Frank robot and wife, that whole bunch of lovesick mechs wanted me to do the job for them, too. Big copper work robots, small aluminum sales-girl mechs, plastoid clerks and typists, squatty little Mumetal lab servos, rationaloids, non-rationaloids and just plain sub-robots—all sizes and shapes. They all wanted individual ceremonies, too. It took till noon the next day before the last couple was hitched and the 990 left for Alinda.

Like I said, the spotel business isn't so different from the motel game back in California. Sure, you got improvements to make but a new sideline can get to be pretty profitable—if you get in on the ground floor.

Min and I got to thinking of all those robot colonizers who'd be coming out here. Interplanetary cleared the license just last week. Min framed it herself and hung it next to our orbit license in the Renting Office. She says a lot of motel owners do all right as Justices of the Peace.